This Book Belongs to

_____

_____

_____

_____

En-joy
Kay A. Eaton

AuthorHouse™
1663 Liberty Drive
Bloomington, IN 47403
www.authorhouse.com
Phone: 1-800-839-8640

First published by AuthorHouse   5/4/2011

ISBN: 978-1-4567-4075-7 (sc)

Library of Congress Control Number: 2011902412

Printed in the United States of America

Any people depicted in stock imagery provided by Thinkstock are models,
and such images are being used for illustrative purposes only.
Certain stock imagery © Thinkstock.

This book is printed on acid-free paper.

authorHOUSE®

Gleason and the Dewdrop's Dream

Kay A. Eaton
Illustrated by Shelly Evans

Inside every dewdrop is a rainbow waiting to be born, and today is Ruby's birthday!

The orchid was the perfect place for her to be seen by the Dewdrop Patrol. She balanced on the tip of the petal and checked the African horizon to be sure she was in the best place to be seen by the sunbeams. She shivered with excitement waiting for the rooster to crow.

"I hear it," she whispered. "The sunbeams will sweep across the landscape any minute now!"

Without warning the orchid began shaking and Ruby could feel herself sliding off the petal.

"What's happening?" she screamed.

Hitting the ground she cried out, "Oh, no! The Dewdrop Patrol won't find me down here! I will never be a rainbow!"

Gleason, the young giraffe, was unaware he bumped the flower causing Ruby to fall.

Hearing strange noises coming from beneath the flowers, he slowly pushed his nose through the petals.

Ruby was frightened by the big animal looking down on her!

"Who . . . who are you?" she asked, her voice quivering.

"My name is Gleason," he answered proudly.

Wiping the tiny tears from Ruby's eyes he asked, "Why are you crying?"

"Today is my birthday. The Dewdrop Patrol was supposed to take me to the Rainbow Ranch so I could learn to be a rainbow," Ruby sobbed.

"I'm sorry..." Gleason said. "I . . . I didn't mean to cause trouble. Can I help?"

"It's too late. They didn't see me and now they are gone. I'll never be a rainbow!" Ruby's tears flowed down her cheeks.

4

Raising his head, Gleason saw the last of the Dewdrop Patrol disappear into the sunlight.

Suddenly he had an idea!

"I have long legs and can run really fast!" he said excitedly. "Come on. We'll catch up with them!"

As carefully as a big giraffe could, Gleason picked up Ruby and began to run.

6

Even running as fast as he could, Gleason realized the Dewdrop Patrol was too far away. He was getting tired but he was determined to get Ruby to the Rainbow Ranch.

Just as he thought he couldn't take another step, he spotted the Ranch.

"We made it, Ruby!"

"Oh, Gleason," Ruby beamed. "Thank you, thank you!"

Putting her tiny arms around him, she kissed him on the cheek.

Gleason's face turned red . . . **very red**.

He waved goodbye to his new friend as she entered the gates of the Ranch.

Ruby promised to come to the gate every day to see him.

Gleason was excited as he waited for Ruby's report.

The first day passed . . . and the second . . . and the third. Gleason thought Ruby had forgotten all about him.

Just as he was about to give up, he heard his name being called. "Gleason! Gleason! Are you there?" Gleason popped his head up over the wall and grinned his biggest grin. "Ruby, you remembered me!"

"I could never forget you, Gleason," she said. "Our classes have kept us very busy."

"What are you learning?" Gleason asked.

"The Stretching and Strengthening class is the hardest. Every day we exercise to build up our muscles so we can reach from horizon to horizon. After that we go to Color Enhancement where we relax while our colors are being perfected. But my favorite class is Purpose and Promise!"

Ruby was excited as she continued, "Long ago, after God created the world, the people were very bad. Instead of loving God they turned against Him. It made God very sad so He began to search for a good man. After looking all over the earth He found Noah and his family.

"God told Noah His plans, 'I'm going to destroy all the earth with a flood. You are to build an ark and when the time is right I will bring animals of all kinds to you. The animals, you, and your family are to enter the ark. I will close the door and it will rain for forty days and nights. I will destroy all that I made. When the flood is over and the land is dry, I will put a rainbow in the sky as My everlasting promise to never destroy the earth with a flood again.' "

Ruby sighed, "Oh, Gleason. When I'm a rainbow people will be happy when they see me because it will remind them of God's promise."

The months passed and Gleason watched Ruby develop into a beautiful rainbow. For awhile she was discouraged because her colors weren't very bright.

"Remember what Professor Sunny Ray said," Gleason reminded her. "When you have a cheerful heart, the colors will have a special glow that will shine brightly for others to see."

Then there were the days she came to the gate leaning to one side or sagging in the middle.

"Oh Gleason," she complained, "Will I ever be strong enough to be a rainbow?"

"Don't give up," encouraged Gleason. "You can do it! One of these days your dream will come true."

Gleason was very proud of Ruby the day her rainbow muscles stretched from horizon to horizon.

When the Placement Patrol called Ruby's name, she was so excited she froze in place!

She heard her name again, "Ruby, come quickly. It's your turn."

Tears came to her eyes. She had trained and learned God's promise and now her dream was about to come true. Her heart was overflowing with joy.

The Placement Patrol motioned her to move faster, "Hurry, Ruby! We don't want to be late!"

As Gleason watched her leave he whispered a prayer, "Please God, help Ruby do her very best."

The Placement Patrol breathed a sigh of relief as they arrived at their destination. "We made it. The storm is almost over."

15

As the storm clouds parted, people could see Ruby high in the sky.

"What a beautiful rainbow!" she heard them say. "It reaches from horizon to horizon!"

Unnoticed by anyone were two thunderclouds hovering nearby. They were jealous that rainbows got all the attention.

"Time to get even!" growled one thundercloud as he glared at Ruby.

While the people were admiring Ruby, the two thunderclouds quickly swept past her and sprayed her with bleach!

Ruby was horrified when she saw her colors disappearing. Her dream was ruined!

Gleason saw what was
happening and ran faster than
ever before to his friend.

"Ruby!" yelled Gleason. "Ruby,
I'm here!"

"Oh, Gleason, what am I going to do? Those thunderclouds sprayed me with
bleach and now my colors are fading," she sobbed.

Suddenly Ruby saw tiny sparkles in her tears that were falling to the ground.

"Colors!" she shouted. "Look at the colors in my tears! Help me put them
back in my rainbow."

Soon all the sunbeams were collecting her tears and putting them where they belonged. Being very tall Gleason was able to reach her highest point and soon Ruby was getting brighter and brighter.

Gleason smiled as he looked at his friend. She was a beautiful rainbow.

She reached from horizon to horizon and her colors were glowing.

Ruby's dream had come true

because . . .

inside every teardrop is a rainbow waiting to be born!

CPSIA information can be obtained
at www.ICGtesting.com
Printed in the USA
LVIC040516160312

273305LV00001B